T0277069

The Wood
at Midwinter

SUSANNA CLARKE

The Wood
at Midwinter

ILLUSTRATED BY
Victoria Sawdon

BLOOMSBURY CIRCUS
LONDON · OXFORD · NEW YORK · NEW DELHI · SYDNEY

It was winter,

just a few days before
Christmas. A few flakes
of snow fell on the quiet
fields. Along the lane that
led to the wood came a
carriage, driven by a young
woman. Her name was
Ysolde Scot and her sister,
Merowdis, sat at her side.

It was a two-wheeled chaise, rather old fashioned and very much in need of a new coat of paint. In the back, two dogs and a russet-coloured pig were looking out at the passing scene with every evidence of enjoyment.

The pig, whose name was Apple, was the subject of conversation. Merowdis was speaking. People would say later — people who remembered her — that her voice sounded young for her age, which was nineteen. It was a sweet, clear, childish voice, at odds with her long, pale, medieval face and plain way of dressing. 'Do you know what Papa said to me? He said, Oh, I know why you called it Apple — because of apple sauce! I didn't understand him at first.'

'He didn't!' said Ysolde. 'Oh, how dreadful! Oh, Apple,' she half turned towards the pig in the back of the carriage, 'I'm so sorry! Don't listen!'

'She's heard it before,' said Merowdis in a resigned sort of way. 'She's only too used to it.'

It must be said that, indignant as the sisters were on her behalf, Apple herself did not seem in the least distressed.

Merowdis and Ysolde's parents did not love Merowdis's animals: not the two dogs presently in the carriage, nor the other six at home. Not the pig, nor the impossible-to-pin-down number of cats. Nor the ferret. Nor the parrot. Nor the wild birds that flew in and out of the house and left their excrements on expensive furnishings. Nor the spiders that gathered in Merowdis's bedroom and which Merowdis refused to let anyone disturb.

'Poor Papa!' said Ysolde. 'He was trying, you see. He was doing his best to understand and be friends with you. Saints are difficult people to live with.'

'Saints!' said Merowdis, rather alarmed at this. 'I never thought of Papa as a saint before!'

'I meant you,' said Ysolde.

'Me!'

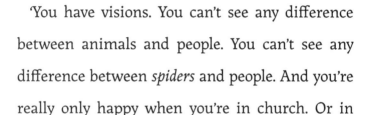

'You have visions. You can't see any difference between animals and people. You can't see any difference between *spiders* and people. And you're really only happy when you're in church. Or in a wood.'

'A church is a sort of wood,' said Merowdis, musingly. 'A wood is a sort of church. They're the same thing really.'

'There!' said Ysolde. 'You see! You say saintly things like that. And no one has any idea what you're talking about.'

The two horses, who knew this journey well, stopped at the wood-gate without any prompting from Ysolde.

'We're here!' said Ysolde. 'Now do put on your bonnet or your head will get cold.'

Merowdis's parents and friends believed that no young lady ought to walk alone in the woods. A woman alone was in danger from all sorts of predatory creatures — bears, wolves, men. Yet walking in the wood was the only thing that interested Merowdis. So Ysolde invented visits for them to make; and then she drove Merowdis to the wood-gate and went on the visits by herself. In a large family Ysolde and Merowdis were each other's favourite sister.

Merowdis, the dogs and the pig got down.

As the sound of the carriage died away, Merowdis sighed. 'Oh, she's gone at last. Good. I love her dearly. She puts up with me. She defends me to Papa and Mama and the others. But her presence is a weight on me. More and more I find it so. It's much better when it's just us.'

Exactly who Merowdis was referring to when she said 'just us' wasn't clear. The dogs and Apple assumed she meant them. The trees were quite sure she was addressing them. A spider making a web in a patch of bramble thought she must be addressing him and that this was, in some sense, an overture of friendship. In reply he left off the first web and began another, the second web being a well-argued treatise on the importance of friendship and what friends owed each other.

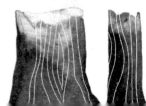

That Merowdis could not read what he had written, indeed was not capable of distinguishing it from any other spider web in the woods, did not occur to him. (If you ever get a chance to learn what is written in spider webs, take it. Spiders have been writing since the world began and know many interesting things.)

The bonnet, which Ysolde had insisted she put on, restricted Merowdis's field of vision, so she took it off and looked vaguely around for somewhere to hang it. Not finding anywhere, she forgot about it and it fell to the ground.

Merowdis, the dogs and the pig entered the wood. A thin layer of snow covered the ground. Copper-coloured leaves lay all around, their edges outlined in white frost. In every direction were avenues of bare trees sinking into blue-white, milky mist, punctuated here and there by green-black holly bushes. The air smelt of frost and earth and decomposing leaves.

It was quiet. From time to time a solitary bird sang.

The names of the dogs were Pretty and Amandier. Pretty was a little dog with silky, ivory-coloured fur. He was what people call a lap dog, though this was not at all how he thought of himself. Amandier was a pale hunting dog, fine-boned, rough-coated

and sensitive in nature. *I do hope there's no bears or wolves in this part of the wood today,* she said. *Can you smell wolves?* She was rather an anxious person.

I love wolfies, said Apple happily. *They're so-oo darling!*

Pretty looked at her. *You have odd ideas for a pig,* he said.

Pretty and Amandier ran about, investigating leaves, dead grass and brambles. Apple applied herself to the more serious business of finding things to eat. *There's always something,* she said. *You just have to smell. I like to put my snout right down into the earth. It smells lovely and I find all sorts of surprises.*

After an hour Merowdis plumped herself down on the snowy ground. Pretty, Amandier and Apple stopped what they were doing and ran into her arms. Tongues licked her face and Apple gave her snuffly, snorting kisses that smelt of the earth.

'Oh, friends!' said Merowdis. 'What am I to do? What am I to *do*? I wanted to be a nun, but the Abbess says I have no aptitude for obedience. Which is true, I suppose. But I cannot marry George Blanchland.' She paused, then asked in a tone of incredulity, 'Can I? I know he wants to marry me, but why? Why? The things I think are important he doesn't care about at all. But if I don't marry George...' She left the thought unfinished.

We know. We know, said Amandier and Pretty. *Don't think about sad things in the wood.*

Look at our lovely and loving faces, said Apple. *Be comforted!*

Two other creatures entered the part of the wood where they were: a blackbird and a fox. The blackbird flew to a nearby branch; the fox watched them warily from between an elder bush and a patch of bramble.

Pretty did not care one way or the other about the blackbird but he greatly objected to the fox; he barked furiously.

'No, no, Pretty,' insisted Merowdis. 'Do not bark at little brother.'

Pretty reluctantly fell silent.

You are in my house now, said the fox. *Be polite.*

I'm terribly sorry, said Pretty airily. *I don't speak fox. Be careful, Amandier. A very low creature is trying to talk to us.*

'In winter,' said Merowdis, lost in her thoughts, 'the wood is supposed to be asleep. That is what people say. But I don't think it's true. In spring and summer the trees and creatures are preoccupied. Everyone is busy. In winter there is silence.'

There *was* silence. But not an empty silence.

'In winter the wood is listening,' said Merowdis.

The blackbird cocked his head and fixed his bright eye on them. The fox took a step nearer.

'In winter you hear the wood speaking,' said Merowdis.

A little wind made the copper leaves rattle. It caught up the snow and sent white eddies and twists snaking away across the ground.

'What I wanted to tell you,' said Merowdis (though it was by no means clear who she was talking to), 'was that what I want above all is a child of my own. Sometimes I feel as if I can hardly think of anything else.' She was silent a moment.

'Of course
it is Christmas
and that makes
me think of
it more.'

Christmas? said the wood.

Its voice was like the wind,
but also like a thousand trees
thinking the same thought.

'The birth of a child,' said Merowdis.
'It happens at this time.'

A human child? asked the wood.

'Yes, a human child,'
said Merowdis.

21

Men are foolish, said the wood.
Have babies in the spring. Not midwinter.
How can babies grow when the earth is frozen?

hen the light is short and the dark is long?

I agree, said the fox.

How can you make milk for babies

when dinner is nothing but skin and bones

and half asleep? Dinner needs to be

mewling and fighting back.

The red blood makes

the yellow

milk.

23

The blackbird did not speak, but he sang a few questioning notes.

'Oh,' said Merowdis, 'but don't you see? The child must come in midwinter. A midwinter child in the arms of a Virgin. A child to bring light into the darkness. A child to heal all wounds.'

Ah! said the wood. *We know what you mean now. You speak of the Sun. The hidden Sun. The Sun in everything.*

'Yes. The hidden Sun,' agreed Merowdis.

Did they say Sun or Son? asked Pretty.

What? said Amandier.

Never mind, said Pretty.

'But the hidden Sun is not enough for me any longer,' said Merowdis. 'I want a child of my own. To hold. To be mine. That is what I wanted to tell you. That is the sorrow I wanted to bring to you.'

Another silence.

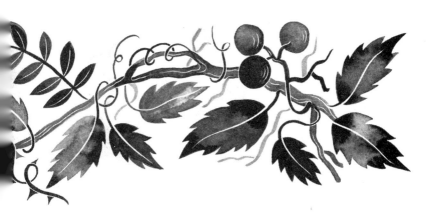

The wood said,

All woods join up with all other woods.

All are one wood.

And in that wood all times

join up with all other times.

All is one moment.

'Yes,' said Merowdis. 'I have thought that before. Or at least I have come close to thinking it.'

And in that one moment,

we see a woman walking.

If you ask me, said Pretty, interrupting hurriedly, *this is not a safe conversation to have. I think we should go.*

Yes, dear mistress, said Amandier. *The daylight is starting to fade. Let's go home to the fireside and the blankets.*

But Merowdis leaned forward and gazed into the darkening trees. 'Show me the woman walking,' she said.

A cloud passed overhead. Grey snow began to fall. It fell faster and faster, and in the midst of the whirling, dizzying flakes a dark figure could be perceived. It had sodden, ragged skirts. It was wrapped in a half-unravelled, black woollen shawl.

Step by step it came on, deliberate but slow, as if in exhaustion. Its hair was wild and loose, caught by the wind, a fire of black flames in the confusion of air and snow.

Pretty began to bark in warning and terror.

Apple turned to Merowdis. *Don't look at it, my dear. Look away. Look at me instead. Look at my happy face. Feel my rough hair.*

Don't look at the terrible thing.

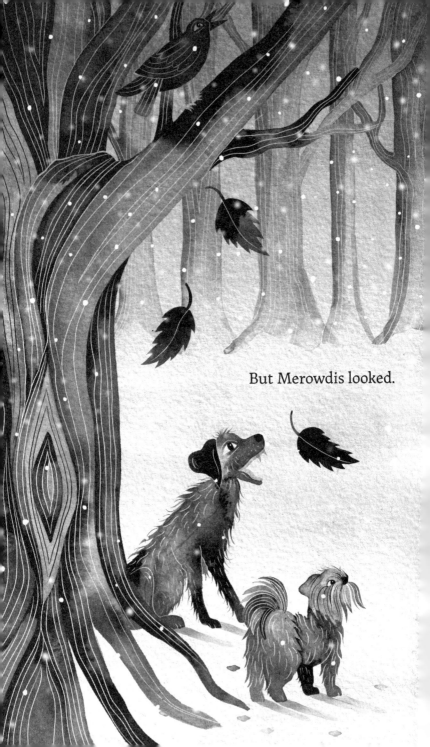

But Merowdis looked.

'The Virgin and the midwinter child,' she said in a wondering tone. 'Oh, but no! It's *me*. *Me* with the midwinter child in my arms.'

The little, wriggling thing that the figure carried did not resemble any child in a painting of the Madonna. It was covered in brown-black fur and had strong claws that had already torn flesh and skin.

'A bear,' said Merowdis. 'A cub! It lost its mother! It needed me!'

She looked! She looked! said Pretty. *And now it will come true!*

She doesn't understand, said Amandier. *She can't understand. Such a love must kill her in the end. Humans aren't meant to live in the woods.*

No, said Apple sadly. *She understands perfectly. Saints do shocking things. It's what makes them saints.*

'Oh, thank you!' cried Merowdis. 'Thank you! Let the little child come to me! I promise I shall love it very much!'

The vision of the woman faded into the snow and at that moment the blackbird began to sing.

I blame you! said Pretty, turning on the fox. *I knew all along you were a bad person. I was right about you!*

The lady is coming to us, said the fox, with a princely lift of his head. *She belongs to us now!*

I hate you! barked Pretty.

The fox turned and vanished into the trees.

Merowdis knelt down and put her arms around Pretty, Amandier and Apple. 'Oh, friends. Dear friends,' she said. 'Don't be sad. We have time. We have time together until my little child comes to me.'

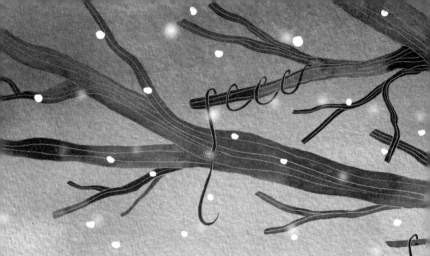

At the gate of the wood, Ysolde was waiting with the carriage. She climbed down from the chaise and picked up Merowdis's bonnet from the snowy ground. She had bought it as a present for Merowdis. Ysolde's allowance was not large and it had been expensive. She sighed. 'One should be patient with saints, I suppose. Though the trouble with being patient,' she said, 'is that, generally speaking, there's no one to see you doing it.'

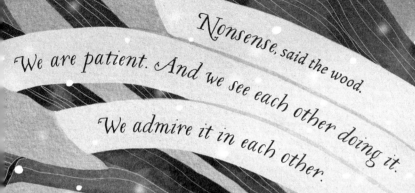

Nonsense, said the wood.

We are patient. And we see each other doing it.

We admire it in each other.

'Home now,' said Ysolde, as Merowdis and the animals walked up. 'Did you enjoy yourself?'

'The wood has promised me a child of my own,' said Merowdis. 'I am so happy, Ysolde.'

'How lovely,' said her sister.

'The world will be cold when my child comes,' explained Merowdis earnestly. 'It will be bitter cold and there will be pain. But you must not be frightened for me because I will have joy — the same joy the Virgin had in the midwinter child.'

'Why would you be cold simply because you have a child? I'm not sure you've quite understood about babies, Merowdis.'

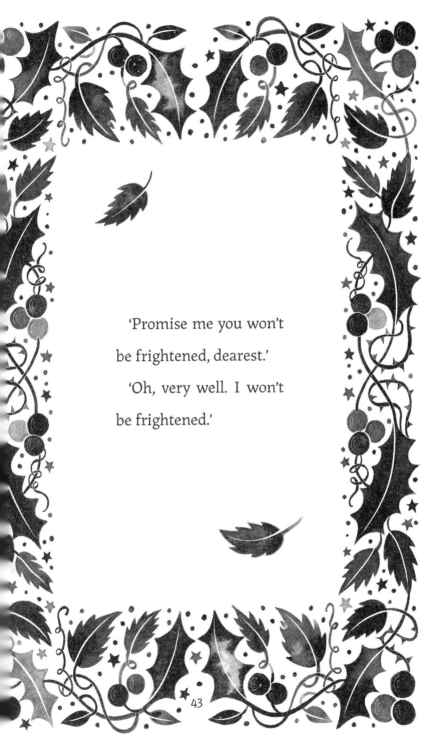

'Promise me you won't
be frightened, dearest.'
'Oh, very well. I won't
be frightened.'

But of course it was not true. The day came when Merowdis disappeared into the wood forever, and Ysolde was very frightened. How could she not be?

Perhaps one day you will visit the city that is near to the wood. Look for the little church that is dedicated to St Francis. In a side chapel, above an altar, you will find a painting of Merowdis Scot.

It shows her seated in a winter wood. Snow falls on her, the wind buffets her, and the dark trees are like the stalls of a savage cathedral. Her throne is black and battered. Her black Victorian dress is ragged. She holds in her lap her child, the brown bear cub. Her expression is fierce,

but also triumphant

Afterword: Snow

IN 2020 MY NOVEL *PIRANESI* WAS PUBLISHED, and, as is the way, people asked me questions about the story and about the world described in the book. I talked about other fiction that I felt had influenced *Piranesi*, and in particular about 'The Library of Babel' by Jorge Luis Borges (a story in which the entire world is, unsurprisingly, a library).

But there is another story by Borges — not perhaps as well known — called 'The House of Asterion'. I had mentioned it in a couple of interviews, but hadn't actually read it since my twenties, about three decades before. So I read it again. Just to see.

It's a story of the original labyrinth in Crete and its inhabitant, the Minotaur. I was astonished how much of that story — elements that I did not consciously remember — had resurfaced in *Piranesi*: the vacant rooms; the human remains which lie scattered in the galleries; the Minotaur's declaration that the house is the world; the way in which he pretends to himself that he is showing the house to someone else and imagines their conversation; his expectation that one day another person will appear in the house to save him.

Sometimes new stories are just old stories badly remembered.

Another example. Throughout my life I have been obsessed with the music of Kate Bush. She and I are almost of an age — I was still a teenager in 1970s Bradford when she began with *The Kick Inside*. Some of the earliest material that became *Jonathan Strange and Mr Norrell* was written while listening to *Hounds of Love*. (There still remains the faintest trace of the song 'Under Ice' in the book, when Strange is being carried through Venice in a gondola and a white glove floating in the water makes him think of a woman under the water, fighting to get back to the light.) In the 2000s I listened over and over to *Aerial*, the second half of which is a great Hymn to Summer.

And then, because she is Kate Bush and the universe requires that she bring balance to it, in 2011 she released *50 Words for Snow*.

And I thought: 'Ah, yes, winter. That is my time.'

I listened obsessively to *50 Words for Snow*, and at some point — I don't remember when exactly — it came to me that the first three songs are all versions of the same story. In each one a woman loves intensely, passionately; but in each one the object of her love is not human. In fact, in two of the songs the beloved is not even an animate creature — at least not in the way we usually think of these things.

In 'Snowflake' a million snowflakes fall over a forest, but the woman sings to just one and that one sings back to her. Over and over the snowflake tells her: 'I'm coming to you'; and over and over she promises: 'I'm waiting for you'. It falls ecstatically through the air into her hands.

In 'Lake Tahoe' a woman calls out to a lost dog, while the dog runs frantically through the dark, snowy wood. In the final part of the song they are reunited and they go through their house together, room by room, looking at all the pieces of their shared life. There is nothing extraordinary

★

here; everything is perfectly mundane, but each room or item signifies love.

In 'Misty' a snowman climbs into a woman's bedroom and becomes her lover. In the morning when he is gone, she follows him out of the window – out onto the ledge. Brought up against the knife-blade of the cold, her reason seems to shred itself into tatters and to be carried away by the wind and the snow.

Some stories sink down into your bones.

In my own writing I had become fascinated by characters who are bridges between different worlds, between different states of being, characters who feel compelled to try and reconcile the unreconcilable. (Such an endeavour must, inevitably, bring certain losses.) An idea formed: the story of a woman who abandons everything to become the mother of a bear cub, and, in doing so, attempts to heal the great estrangement between the natural world and Man.

Yet, just as before, I wasn't consciously aware of any connection between the woman with the bear cub, and the women from *50 Words for Snow*, with their unwavering pursuit of inhuman loves; until, one day, I listened to the album again, and suddenly there were all the elements of Merowdis's story laid out in front of me: wind; woods; animals; snow; the insistence that the category of things we love could be larger; and a woman who is so single-minded in following where love leads that she barely notices she has left sanity behind. If you think about it, Kate Bush has been singing about this same woman — or a version of her — since 'Wuthering Heights'.

Take that woman, give her psychology just a little twist and she is not so very far from the

★

people we call saints. Saints are not very well understood any longer. We think of them as living lives that are limited, lives of pointless self-denial, when the truth is almost the opposite: saints are often frighteningly free. As Apple the pig remarks, 'Saints do shocking things. It's what makes them saints.'

Nowadays we would probably call Merowdis neuro-divergent. She has long since given up the idea that anyone else will understand the things that are important to her. She has a little bit of my dad in her. He believed that he had Asperger's syndrome, though he was never diagnosed. He once said to me: 'I know that other people are not interested in the things that I am interested in.'

By the time Elizabeth Allard, a producer at BBC Radio 4, asked me for a story to be broadcast just before Christmas 2022, I was ready to write about

Merowdis. I included the wood not as a setting but as a character. The wood speaks because a tree is a kind of person. Trees exist on a different timescale from us, but they have certain sorts of thoughts and a certain way of looking at the world. I have believed this since I was a child. The snow is there because it is a Christmas story, but also because snow always seems to me to signal a quietening of the spirit, a different sort of consciousness. And then obviously I added a pig, because there ought to be more pigs in books.

My last thought concerns Merowdis's whereabouts, her actual physical location. She seems to be in England — or possibly Scotland or Wales. But this is misleading. Merowdis belongs to the world of Jonathan Strange and Mr Norrell.

I am fairly certain that *Jonathan Strange and Mr Norrell* contained at one time a long footnote

with a careful explanation of Merowdis's city —
the city that is near the wood, the city where she
lives. I had intended to refer you to that footnote,
so that you could find out all about it (how it is
very beautiful, how it was built in the twelfth
century by John Uskglass, the King of the North,
and William Lanchester, his chancellor, etc. etc.).
But I cannot do that because the footnote has
vanished. I imagine that some fairy has removed
it for reasons of his or her own. (Fairies are like
that.)

All you need to know is that Merowdis's city is
the King's capital of Newcastle.

But not that Newcastle.

The other one.

Susanna Clarke

MAY 2024

BLOOMSBURY PUBLISHING
Bloomsbury Publishing Inc.
1385 Broadway, New York, NY 10018, USA

BLOOMSBURY, BLOOMSBURY PUBLISHING, and the Diana logo are trademarks of
Bloomsbury Publishing Plc

A version of this story was read on BBC Radio 4 in 2022
First published in 2024 in Great Britain
First published in the United States 2024

Library of Congress Cataloging-in-Publication Data is available

ISBN: HB: 978-1-63973-448-1; eBook: 978-1-63973-449-8

4 6 8 10 9 7 5 3

Typeset and designed by Goldy Broad
Printed and bound in the U.S.A.

To find out more about our authors and books visit www.bloomsbury.com
and sign up for our newsletters.

Bloomsbury books may be purchased for business or promotional use. For information on bulk
purchases please contact Macmillan Corporate and Premium Sales Department at
specialmarkets@macmillan.com.